Angryman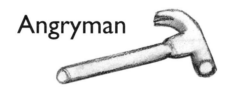

This translation has been published with the financial support of NORLA.

**A big thank-you to family therapist Øivind Aschjem, who took the initiative with this book,
and to psychologist Solveig Karin Bø Vatnar and the project Witness to Violence.**

First published in the United States, Great Britain, Canada, Australia, and New Zealand in 2019 by NorthSouth Books Inc.,
an imprint of NordSüd Verlag AG, CH-8050 Zürich, Switzerland.

Distributed in the United States by NorthSouth Books Inc., New York 10016.
Library of Congress Cataloging-in-Publication Data is available.
ISBN: 978-0-7358-4340-0
Printed in Latvia
1 3 5 7 9 • 10 8 6 4 2
www.northsouth.com

ANGRYMAN

Gro Dahle • Svein Nyhus
Translated by Tara Chace

North
South

Boj is listening. There's something in the living room. It's Daddy.

Is Daddy quiet? Is Daddy happy? Is Daddy calm?

Yes. Daddy's calm now. Now Daddy's happy!

See how happy Daddy is! He's as cheerful as apples on the table and raisins in a yellow bowl. Cheerful as a bag of lemon drops and a three-layer birthday cake with candles on top. Cheerful! Cheerful as some presents tied up with ribbons and a glass of soda with a straw. Cheerful as apple pie.

Mama's laughing in her finest dress.

"My daddy," Boj says, looking at Daddy. Big, big, cheerful Daddy. Daddy's hands are so big. Daddy's hands have red knuckles.

My daddy, Boj thinks, looking at Daddy.

I might be as big as Daddy someday, Boj thinks.

Daddy is quiet.

Boj looks at Daddy. Why is Daddy quiet now? Is Daddy tired?

Is Daddy worn-out? Is Daddy angry? Everything is so delicate. The whole living room is made of glass. Everything is swaying. Because something's in the living room. It's Daddy.

And Daddy is quiet.

Something's creeping out from the corners. Something's waiting in the wall. Shadows in the wallpaper. A cupboard that's open just a crack. Vases getting ready to fall. "*Shh*, close the doors carefully. *Shh*, walk quietly across the floor. Clear the glasses from the table."

Is Daddy in the living room now?

"*Shh*," Mama says, even though Boj isn't saying anything.

"Be quiet," Mama says.

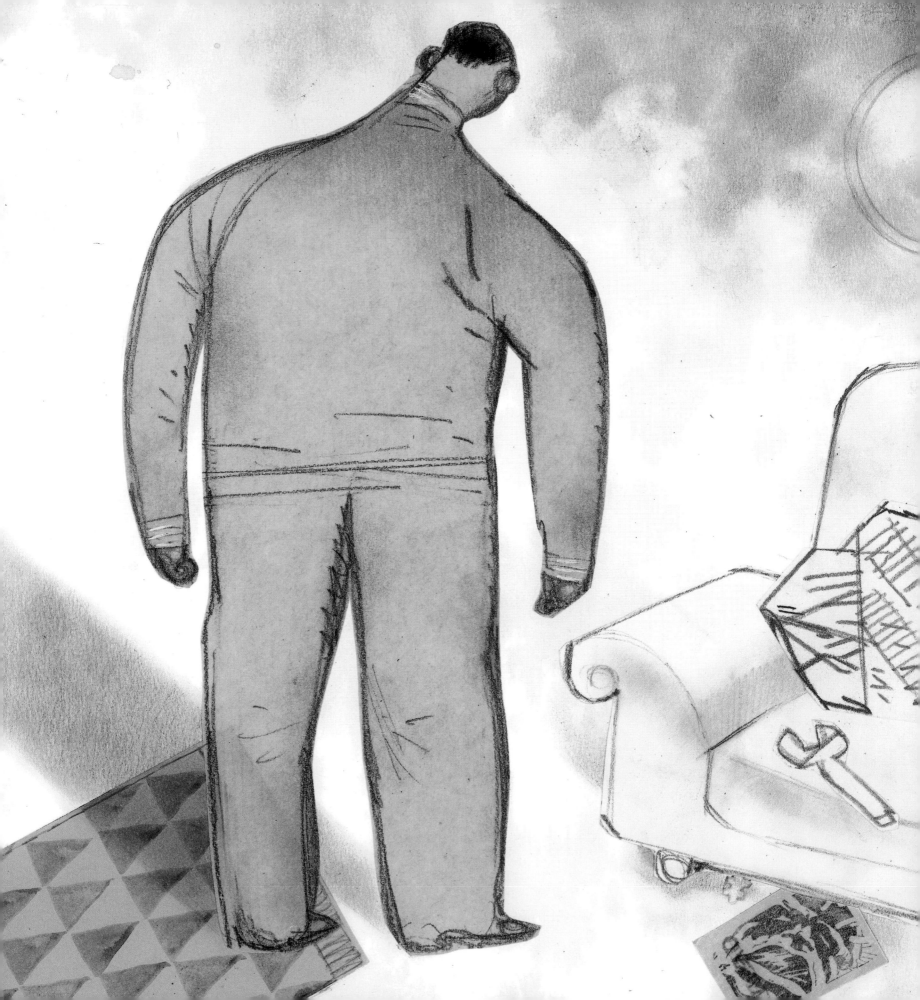

There's something in the living room. It's Daddy. There's something in the house. It's Daddy. Boj feels something tighten. Boj's hands hurt. And Boj's heart starts to race. The race inside Boj is catching up with him.

Mama takes Boj into her arms. Mama says something with her mouth.

"*Shh,* Mama, *shh.* Don't let your mouth talk."

Mama sets Boj on her lap. Boj's leg is trembling. Because Daddy is sitting in his chair and pulling the curtains in his eyes. He closes off his face.

Why is Daddy like that? Boj thinks. *Was it something I did? Was it something I said?* Boj wonders, hunkering down inside of himself. *Is Daddy calm now? Is Daddy happy? Is Daddy mad?*

"I'm not mad," Daddy says. "Don't say I'm mad when I'm not mad," he says. The first thing is his voice, the small tone in his voice. It's that little flag. His voice tightens more and more. And his voice gets padlocks on it, and sharp edges. "I'm not mad," Daddy says. But behind Daddy's voice, there is a closed door. And behind the door, behind his voice, there is a dark cellar. And down in the cellar, someone is waiting. A bent back. A dark muscle. A neck.

Mama holds Boj tightly on her lap. She strokes and strokes Boj with her hands, and she keeps stroking. And Boj hears the clock chime a hundred chimes.

It's just Daddy. But in that cellar behind Daddy's voice, someone is coming up. And someone is coming up the stairs inside Daddy. Boj hears it in his breathing. Boj hears it in the steps and in the door that slams. It's Angryman who's coming up Daddy's back. Angryman curling around Daddy's neck. Angryman climbing up ladders of ribs. It's Angryman who wants out.

Oh dear Daddy, don't let Angryman out.

Don't let Angryman come. I'll be so good. I won't say a word. I won't breathe. But Boj hears Angryman coming. Everyone can hear Angryman coming. Angryman is in Daddy's breathing, in his face. In his throat. In his neck.

In his hands and legs. Angryman is everywhere on Daddy. Everyone sees it. Everyone notices it. Everyone. Except for Daddy.

"Daddy needs to rest a little," Mama says, smoothing the tablecloth.

"Daddy has to work hard," Mama says, smoothing the rug.

"Don't bother Daddy now," Mama says, closing the door to Daddy.

Because something's in the living room. It's not Daddy.

It's Angryman.

The room tightens down to the very walls.

Even the ceiling is holding its breath.

"There, there, there, there, there," Mama says.

"There, there, there, there, there, there," Mama says.

Why is Daddy so mad? Boj thinks.

Maybe it's my fault, Boj thinks. *I have to be better. Behave better. Do whatever it takes. Sorry. Sorry. Daddy, Daddy. Nice Daddy.*

Mama takes Boj out with her into the hallway. Angryman follows. Mama takes Boj upstairs with her. Angryman follows. Mama takes Boj with her into the bedroom. Angryman follows.

"Stay in your room, Boj," Mama says. Growing big and wide, she puts herself in the way of Angryman. She puts herself in the way and becomes a barrier. A wall. Woe to him who dares to breathe. Woe to him who has spilled milk on the floor. Woe to him who has said something wrong, something stupid, something that cannot be taken back. Woe to her who stands in the way when Angryman comes.

Stop, Angryman.

Stop.

But nothing can stop Angryman when Angryman comes. Because a door is not a door. A wall is not a wall. And Mama is not Mama. Because nothing can stop Angryman. Boj must not breathe. Boj must not see, must not speak, must not hear. Because Angryman is coming.

"Stay in your room, Boj," Mama says.

"Boj, into your room!"

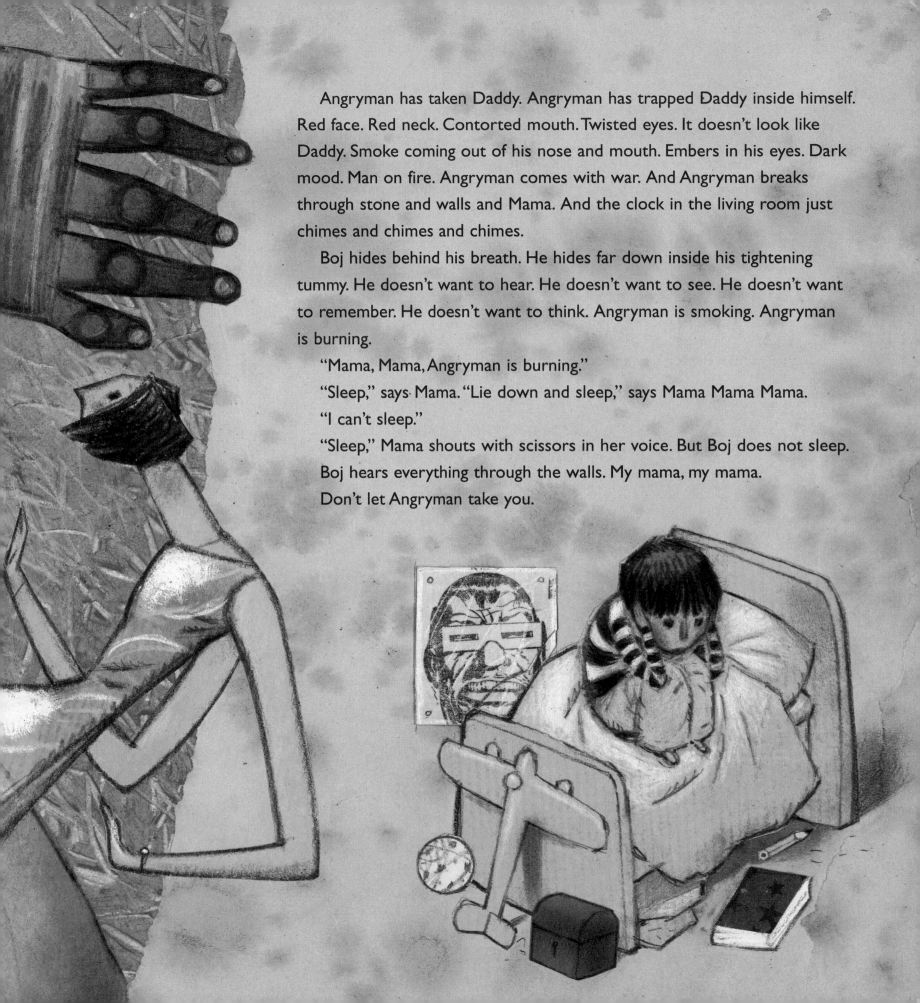

Angryman has taken Daddy. Angryman has trapped Daddy inside himself. Red face. Red neck. Contorted mouth. Twisted eyes. It doesn't look like Daddy. Smoke coming out of his nose and mouth. Embers in his eyes. Dark mood. Man on fire. Angryman comes with war. And Angryman breaks through stone and walls and Mama. And the clock in the living room just chimes and chimes and chimes.

Boj hides behind his breath. He hides far down inside his tightening tummy. He doesn't want to hear. He doesn't want to see. He doesn't want to remember. He doesn't want to think. Angryman is smoking. Angryman is burning.

"Mama, Mama, Angryman is burning."

"Sleep," says Mama. "Lie down and sleep," says Mama Mama Mama.

"I can't sleep."

"Sleep," Mama shouts with scissors in her voice. But Boj does not sleep. Boj hears everything through the walls. My mama, my mama.

Don't let Angryman take you.

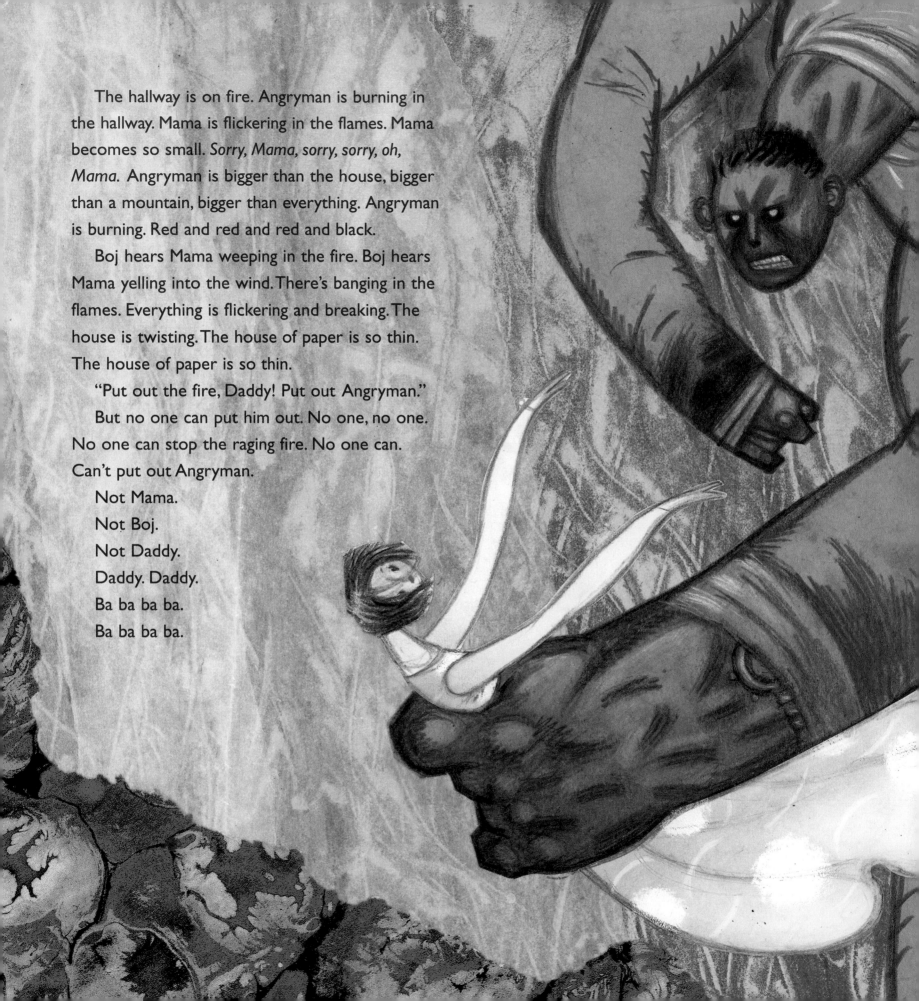

The hallway is on fire. Angryman is burning in the hallway. Mama is flickering in the flames. Mama becomes so small. *Sorry, Mama, sorry, sorry, oh, Mama.* Angryman is bigger than the house, bigger than a mountain, bigger than everything. Angryman is burning. Red and red and red and black.

Boj hears Mama weeping in the fire. Boj hears Mama yelling into the wind. There's banging in the flames. Everything is flickering and breaking. The house is twisting. The house of paper is so thin. The house of paper is so thin.

"Put out the fire, Daddy! Put out Angryman."

But no one can put him out. No one, no one. No one can stop the raging fire. No one can. Can't put out Angryman.

Not Mama.

Not Boj.

Not Daddy.

Daddy. Daddy.

Ba ba ba ba.

Ba ba ba ba.

Ba ba ba ba.

Ba ba.

Ba.

Ba.

Beyond a ridge of blue mountains. Beyond thought. Barefoot in the grass.

Where Boj is running with a white dog. Where Boj is running barefoot in the grass.

"Let's go for a walk!" Boj yells.

And the white dog barks and laughs. Barking and laughing.

Ha-ha ho-ho.
Ha-ha ho-ho.

Boj dances with the dog.

He's a curly haired white poodle. Good dog.

Soot and ash in the air. Soot and ash. But the dog jumps and laughs.

Ha-ha.

Soot and ash. Gray soot and ash. Tears and soot and ash. The fire has burned up Angryman. Angryman has become thin flakes in the wind. Angryman has become dust and earthworms and snails and vanishes into the ground. He vanishes into the muck and dirt. He crawls back down Daddy's crooked spine. It's just Daddy sitting there again. Poor Daddy. Poor big Little Daddy. Stump-like. Poor stumpy. Stumpy old man, shuffly old man. Shuffle Daddy. Ba ba ba.

Daddy looks where Angryman has been. He looks at the smashed bowl; he looks at the mark on the wall; he looks at the ruined door. He looks at Mama. And Daddy looks at Angryman in his own hands.

Now Angryman is deep, deep, down, behind and under, and far, far inside. Down there, Angryman has to crawl in narrow tunnels and hide in closed closets in the cellar.

"I won't be mad anymore," Daddy says. "I won't be bad anymore," Daddy says. "I promise," Daddy says. He can say that because Daddy has said it before. Many times before.

"Poor Daddy," says Mama, taking off her white silk scarves, winding them around Daddy's hands. Daddy's red hands. Daddy's big hands.

"Where does it hurt?" Mama asks.

"There and there and there and there," Daddy says, weeping and weeping. And Mama ties her white silk scarves everywhere it hurts.

Daddy is a sponge that has sucked up the entire ocean. "Hold me," Little Daddy weeps, leaking from all the cracks. And Boj must comfort Daddy and taste Little Daddy's salty tears.

"I'll only be nice," Daddy says. "I promise," Daddy says, breaking into a thousand million tears. And everyone holds Daddy, because otherwise Daddy will wash away. Every wave in the ocean is crying. Crying and crying. You can't see anything underwater. The salty ocean is dark and hundreds and hundreds of feet deeper than deep.

Afterward, it's as quiet as a fly on the ceiling. Afterward, it's as quiet as the pictures on the wall. Afterward, it's as quiet as the water in the pitcher. And no one knows what's living under the carpet. No one knows what's living in the walls.

Boj listens to footsteps and sounds. Every sound is like a growl. And all the sounds are talking about Daddy. There is no Boj. There is no Mama. Daddy is all there is.

Boj's legs are trembling, and Boj cowers and disappears under the tablecloth. *And it's getting hard to breathe*, Boj thinks, and Boj's neck and tummy and head start hurting just thinking that.

Boj wants to get out. He wants to get away.

"Can you unlock the door, Mama?" Boj asks.

"Not now," Mama says. Because Mama has to take care of Daddy and wrap white scarves around his hands. And Boj mustn't talk about it. Mustn't see, mustn't talk, mustn't hear. Because it's secret-secret, and we're doing so well, so well. That's what Mama says. So well, so well.

Because who else would deal with the computer? And who else would fix the car or screw in the lightbulbs? Where else would we live? How would we manage without Daddy?

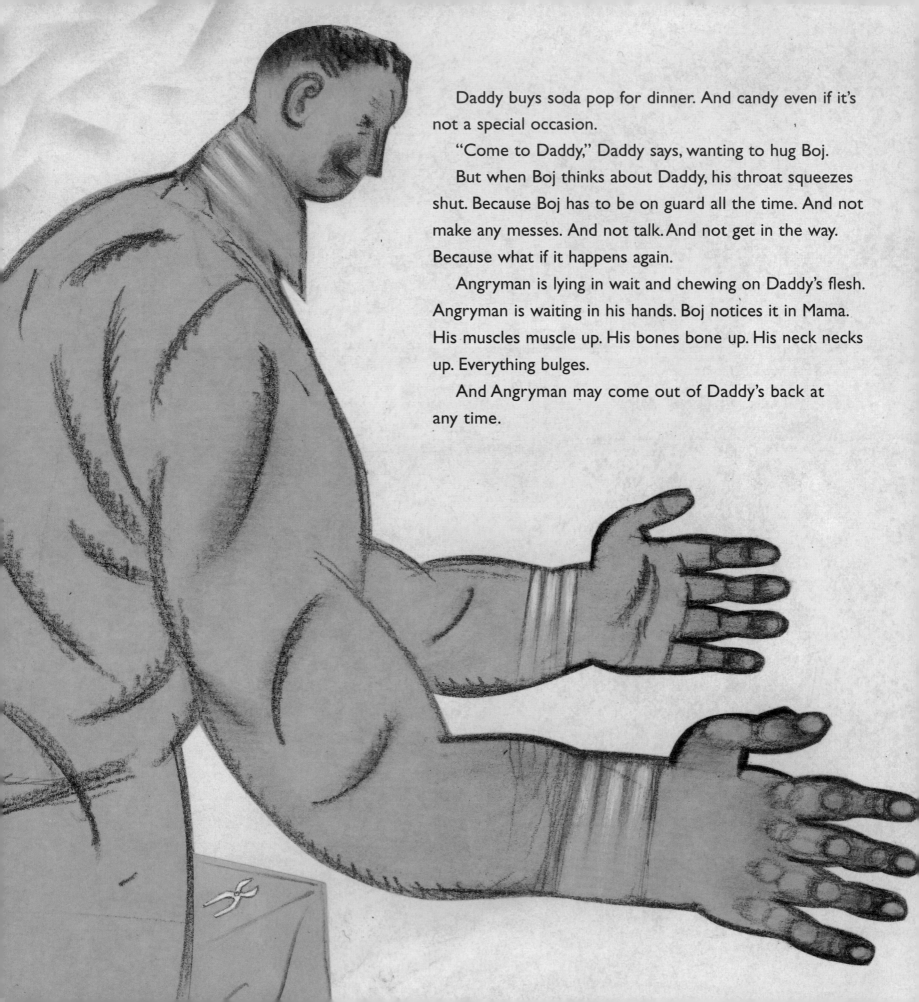

Daddy buys soda pop for dinner. And candy even if it's not a special occasion.

"Come to Daddy," Daddy says, wanting to hug Boj.

But when Boj thinks about Daddy, his throat squeezes shut. Because Boj has to be on guard all the time. And not make any messes. And not talk. And not get in the way. Because what if it happens again.

Angryman is lying in wait and chewing on Daddy's flesh. Angryman is waiting in his hands. Boj notices it in Mama. His muscles muscle up. His bones bone up. His neck necks up. Everything bulges.

And Angryman may come out of Daddy's back at any time.

Mama becomes a chair in the corner. She wants to hold Boj on her lap. But Boj doesn't want to sit. Boj wants out. His shoes are calling impatiently by the door. *Out out out.* His shoes want to run away with him.

"Unlock the door, Mama!" But Mama can't manage to do it; she can't do it. She can't find the keys. There aren't any keys.

"The doors are open, Boj," Mama says. "Just run outside and play," Mama says. But the doors aren't open. The doors are closed for a long way. A thousand doors have shut Boj in. And Mama can't find the keys. Because Mama has no keys to find. Boj must open the doors himself. Unlock the lock within the lock. Open the door within the door. And the door behind the door within the door. Because Boj has to get out. *Out out out.* Boj has to get out. *Get out, Boj. Get away.*

See? The door is open!

There are no locked doors out there.
Everything is open. The only doors there are, are
the doors inside Boj. They're slamming in the wind.

When Boj looks back at the house, the house
is quiet. The windows are closed. They don't even
blink. There's not so much as a flutter in the
curtains. The walls seal tight, board against board.
Not even the smoke escapes the chimney.

But there's something inside. It knows Boj.
It's Daddy.

Boj feels like telling. The words are pounding with lots of little hammers. The words want to get out and whisper and talk and yell. But his mouth is locked again with seven locks, glued again with superglue, and nailed again with a hundred nails. And no matter how many words are screaming inside Boj, they just can't escape. Because Boj can't open his mouth. Boj can't tell. The words are prisoners inside Boj's head.

Boj knows about a lady. She has a red jacket and a big dog. She knows about Boj. And Boj knows that she knows, because the lady has eyeglasses that see really well. They're really strong eyeglasses with really thick lenses. And her dog has such brown eyes.

"Hello, Boj," she says, looking at him through her eyeglasses. "Is everything okay?" she asks.

But Boj can't get his mouth to say anything, because it's locked and glued and nailed shut.

The words are nearly bursting, and they're pushing and pounding, but Boj can't do anything except nod. Because that's all Boj can do. A little nod is all there is.

The dog is sitting by the fence, waiting. The dog licks Boj's hands, and Boj pets the dog's ears. And the dog has such big, soft ears. And the dog listens until the glue on Boj's lips comes unstuck and the words crawl out of his mouth. Herds of words.

Boj tells the dog. And Boj tells the bushes and the birds and the grass and the climbing tree. The tree listens with each and every leaf, carrying Boj way up into the wind and clouds and sky. "Keep saying it," the tree whispers in the wind.

"Say it. Say it."

"I can't," Boj says. "I just can't," Boj says, feeling the weight of the latches and locks.

"Write a letter," the dog says.

"A letter, a letter," sparrows chirp in the thicket.

The clouds struggle across the sky. The wind struggles in the tree. The sparrows struggle in the thicket. The thrushes and starlings call from the lawn. "Say it. Say it. Write a letter. Write a letter."

Then Boj feels something rushing into his hands, and he feels his fingers filling with words. His fingertips are tingling to tell. The letters of the alphabet are tickling under his skin. *Write, write.*

Dear King, Boj writes.

Daddy hits, Boj writes.

Is it my fault? Boj asks.

Sincerely yours, Boj, Boj writes.

Something is tugging at Boj, pulling his hair. The house has dark windows, closed doors, silent boards. But the tree is shouting with joy. "You did it!" the tree calls, lifting Boj up in the air, high up on its shoulders.

It's a day full of birds and wind. It's a day full of leaves and air. It's a day with a knocking on the door. *Knock, knock, knock.*

It's the king.

"Boj!" the king calls.

"Are you there, Boj?" the king calls.

Then all the doors open. And the king can walk right in to find Boj.

"Hello, Boj," the king says. Boj doesn't dare look at Daddy. His tongue lies flat inside his mouth, hiding behind his teeth.

"Well done, Boj," the king says, "and thank you for your letter." And the king has a big crown on. Because only the king is the king.

"It's not your fault, Boj," the king says, shaking his head.

Then the king looks at Daddy. And he says Daddy has to get down on his knees and apologize to Boj.

And Daddy does. Daddy goes down on both knees in front of Boj, becoming smaller than Boj. Now Boj is big, and Daddy is little.

"I'm sorry, Boj," Daddy says.

"It's not your fault," Daddy says. "It's my fault."

"But what should I do with Angryman?" Daddy asks, looking at the king.

"Angryman is so terribly strong," Daddy says.

"But you are stronger," the king says. "And you will come live with me. Because I have many rooms in my castle and a big garden with all kinds of birds."

Boj looks at Daddy. Daddy gets to live with the king. Daddy will get to fix himself there. Because Daddy has to glue the pieces together and sew on the patches. And Daddy has to walk all the way down the long, long staircase to Angryman and get to know him. Listen to Angryman and become his friend. And see that, behind Angryman, there is an old Angryman, an angry grumpy-faced shuffling old man who Daddy also has to talk to.

Daddy will pat Angryman on the back. Daddy will comfort itty-bitty Little Daddy, who is always crying. Daddy will hold them in his hands, take them into his lap, Angryman and itty-bitty Little Daddy and shuffling old man will sit together with Daddy on the grass under the trees and clouds and sky in the king's castle gardens and tell one another stories and comfort one another. And then Angryman won't be dangerous or locked up anymore. Because Daddy will hold him in his hand, look after him. And Little Daddy won't be sad anymore. Because Daddy will pat him on the back. And the words will flow and fly like slender butterflies and stocky bumblebees. And the words will get to crawl like ants and ladybugs. And then Daddy will become whole again.

"That'll be wonderful, won't it?" Daddy says, exhaling a big breath. And Mama smiles, breathes, and smiles.

The king says that Boj can come and visit Daddy as often as he wants. Then Daddy can pick up Boj in the sunshine and roll and roll around and around with Boj in the grass. And the tree will sing with its boughs in the wind. And the king will nod and smile. And the lady next door will watch out of her window through her eyeglasses and see that Boj is doing okay now. And the big white dog by the fence will wag his tail and bark and jump and dance and laugh. Ha-ha hee-hee.

Boj will get to run with the dog and forget everything and just be Boj Boj Boj all day long. Climbing in the tree, swinging on the branches, swinging and jumping. Because someone is under the tree. And it's someone who can take care of him. Someone who's safe.

It's Daddy. Because Daddy will catch Boj when Boj jumps. Daddy will catch his boy.

And Daddy says, "Well done, Boj."

All the doors are wide-open.

Sun and air, and wind in his hair.

Stars in his mouth.

Ha-ha hee-hee.

Hee-hee.

Gro Dahle is a poet and author, born in Oslo, Norway, in 1962. She graduated from the University of Oslo and studied creative writing at Telemark University College. In 1987, she debuted with *Audien*, a poetry collection that was very well received. She has since become a well-known lyricist and novelist. She lives in Tjøme, in Vestfold, with her husband, Svein Nyhus.

Svein Nyhus is an illustrator and writer of children's books, born in Tonsberg, Norway, in 1962. He studied at the Norwegian National Academy of Craft and Art Industry. Among many other book projects, he illustrated *Why Kings and Queens Don't Wear Crowns*, written by Princess Märtha Louise of Norway, and the *New York Times* best seller *What Does the Fox Say?*, based on Ylvis's YouTube hit *The Fox*. He lives in Tjøme, in Vestfold, with his wife, Gro Dahle.